KU-298-358

SCHOOLS LIBRARY SERVICE
MALTBY LIBRARY HEADQUARTERS
HIGH STREET
MALTBY
ROTHERHAM
S66 8LD

SEP 2009

ROTHERHAM LIBRARY & INFORMATION SERVICES

This book must be returned by the date specified at the time of issue
As the DATE DUE for RETURN.
The loan may be extended (personally,by post or telephone) for a
Further period,If the book is not required by another reader,
By quoting the above number/author/title.

LIS 7a

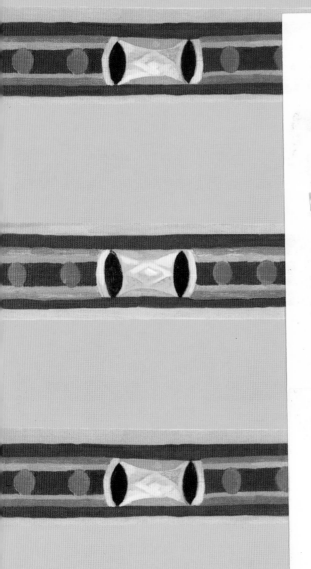
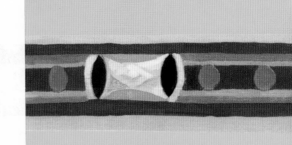

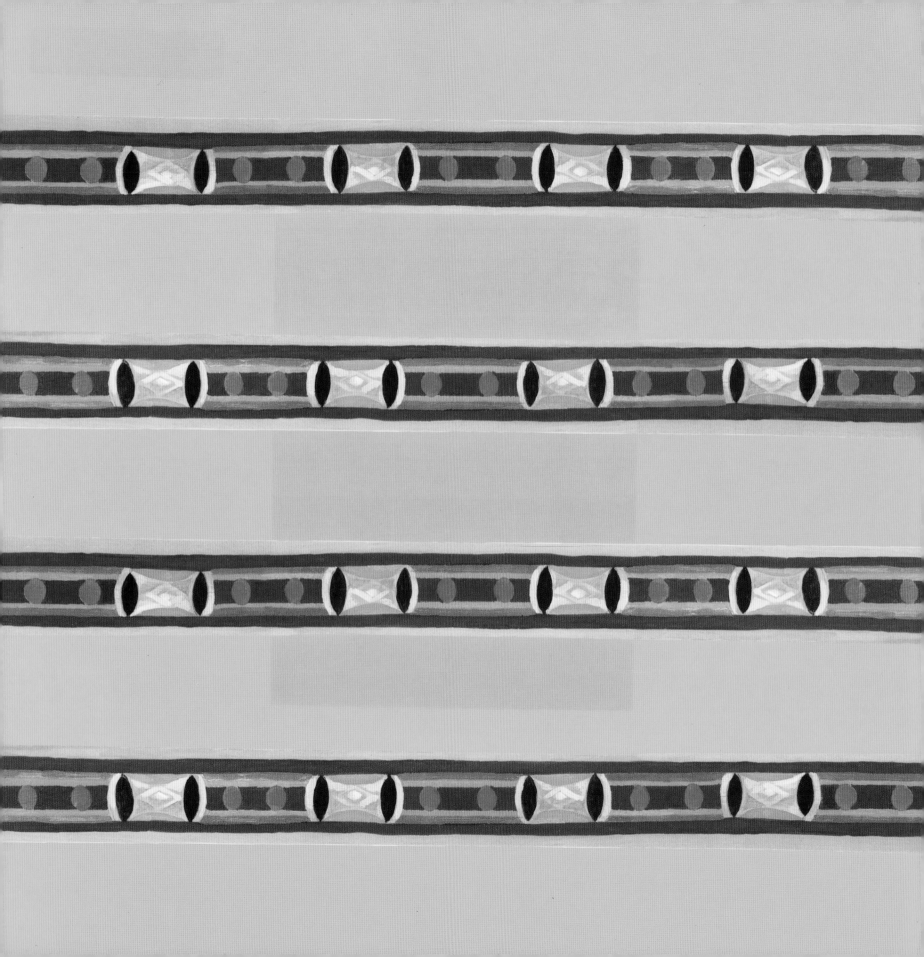

My Little African King

Written & Illustrated by Katherine Roundtree

Black Butterfly Children's Books

My Little African King

Text & Illustrations Copyright © 1999 by Katherine Roundtree
All rights reserved

This book is sold subject to the condition that it shall not, by way of trade or otherwise, be lent, re-sold,
hired out, or otherwise circulated without the publisher's prior consent in any form of binding or
cover other than that in which it is published and without a similar condition
being imposed on the subsequent purchaser.

All rights reserved. No part of this publication may be reproduced, stored in a retrieval system, or transmitted
in any form or by any means, electronic, mechanical, photocopying, recording or otherwise,
without the prior permission of the publisher.

ISBN: 0-86316-249-5

Published by Writers and Readers Publishing, Inc.
for Black Butterfly Books

ROTHERHAM LIBRARY &
INFORMATION SERVICES

B48 046924 2

R00033837

Printed in Hong Kong

When I look into your deep brown eyes,
I see the joy you bring
and think of who you are inside,
My Little African King.

I must tell you of Africa, the great Mother Earth,
the magnificent land of your forefather's birth
and its ancient Kingdoms and land of great worth,
My Little African King.

You possess the wisdom of your fathers,
the Kings of Africa, their sons and daughters.
In their minds great freedom rings,
My Little African King.

See the King's caravans stretch far and wide,
their camels with spices piled high.
Listen to the talking drums speak through the air,
Twangas and flutes sing of harvest fare.

The grasslands of Africa are wild and free,
with lions, elephants, and tall Thorn trees.
The lions rest in the meadows of grass,
while great roaming herds of elephants pass.

The people travel to Timbuktu,
to shop and trade and business do.
They buy ripe vegetables and meat for stew,
and Kente cloth for garments too.

The markets are filled with throngs of people
who travel from far and from near.
The Malinke, the Songhai, the Falani, and Ibo,
the Asante of Ghana come here.

My son, you are great, you are grand, you are bold,
though of your past you have never been told.
Of your great heritage I now will sing,
My Little African King.

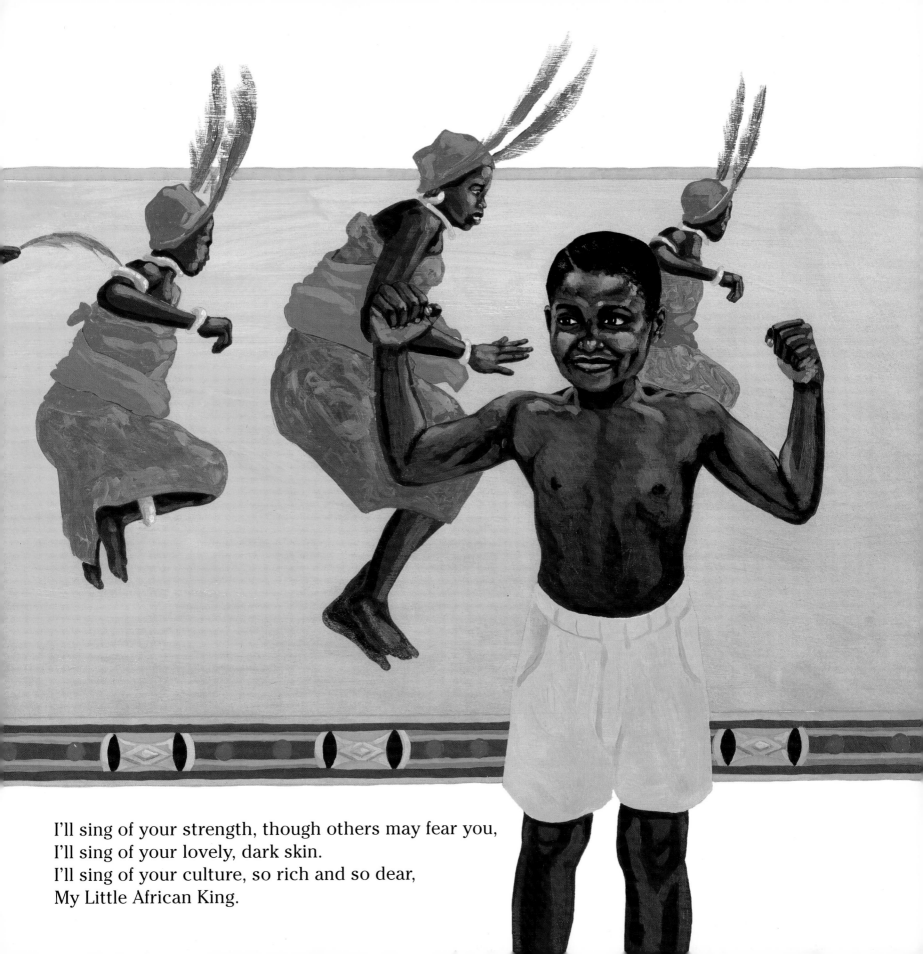

I'll sing of your strength, though others may fear you,
I'll sing of your lovely, dark skin.
I'll sing of your culture, so rich and so dear,
My Little African King.

Mansa Kankan Musa was a powerful King,
his people called him "Black Moses."
He was born of Sundiata, The Lion King,
who conquered Sumanguru, The Susu King,
from Musa's great line you would later spring,
My Little African King.

He wore great robes laced with gold
and possessed a Kingdom of riches untold.
His stature was tall and his presence bold,
My Little African King.

In the land of Africa your name is Oheneba,
descendant of the Mighty King.
It means you are royal, both prosperous and wise,
A Little African King.

Mansa Musa's empire was the greatest of the land,
it stretched both far and wide.
From the salt mines of Taghaza to the copper mines of Kakedda,
to Niger and back again.

Mali is the Kingdom where Musa reigned.
His soldiers were strong, proud warriors.
Their courage and strength to you they gave,
My Little African King.

Your forefathers came from the Madinke land,
a wise and united people.
To peace, prosperity, and learning they cling,
My Little African King.

When Musa entered with his magnificent court
the musicians would lead the way,
with gold and silver two-stringed guitars
and singers ringing their bells and bars.

The crowd would bow and all would hush
as Musa accepted his people's trust.
To his Ivory Throne up the stairs he'd ascend,
My Little African King.

The city was safe for his guards were fierce.
His people had nothing to fear.
Neither thief, nor robber, nor villain came near,
My Little African King.

The richest, most powerful, most generous King,
Mansa Musa ruled everything.
Wisdom and kindness and good he would bring,
My Little African King.

He traveled to Mecca with caravans of gold,
inspiring other great kingdoms to grow.
His riches he left wherever he'd go,
My Little African King.

You were born with his wisdom
I see it in you,
in all that you say and all that you do.
So be creative, go forth, use good judgement and rule,
My Little African King.

And when you are grown with children of your own,
your strength will be their shelter.
To their hearts and minds your great heritage bring,
My Little African King.

No matter how old or how tall you may be,
or how far from home you may roam,
in your precious eyes I'll always see,
My Little African King!

Also available from

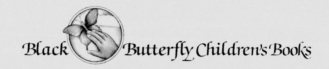

PICTURE BOOKS

By Eloise Greenfield and Jan Spivey Gilchrist

Aaron and Gayla's Alphabet Book
Aaron and Gayla's Counting Book
First Pink Light
Indigo and Moonlight Gold
Nathaniel Talking

By Lorraine Simeon

Marcellus
Marcellus' Birthday Cake

By Katherine Roundtree

My Little African King

By Tom Feelings

Tommy Traveler in the World of Black History

By Sue Adler

Mandela for Young Beginners®

BOARD BOOKS

By Eloise Greenfield and Jan Spivey Gilchrist

Big Friend, Little Friend
I Make Music
My Doll Keshia
My Daddy and I

By Carole Weatherford and Michelle Mills

Grandma and Me
Mighty Menfolk
Me and The Family Tree
My Favorite Toy

By Laura Pegram

Rainbow Is Our Face
A Windy Day

By Paula deJoie

My Hair Is Beautiful . . . Because It's Mine!
My Skin is Brown

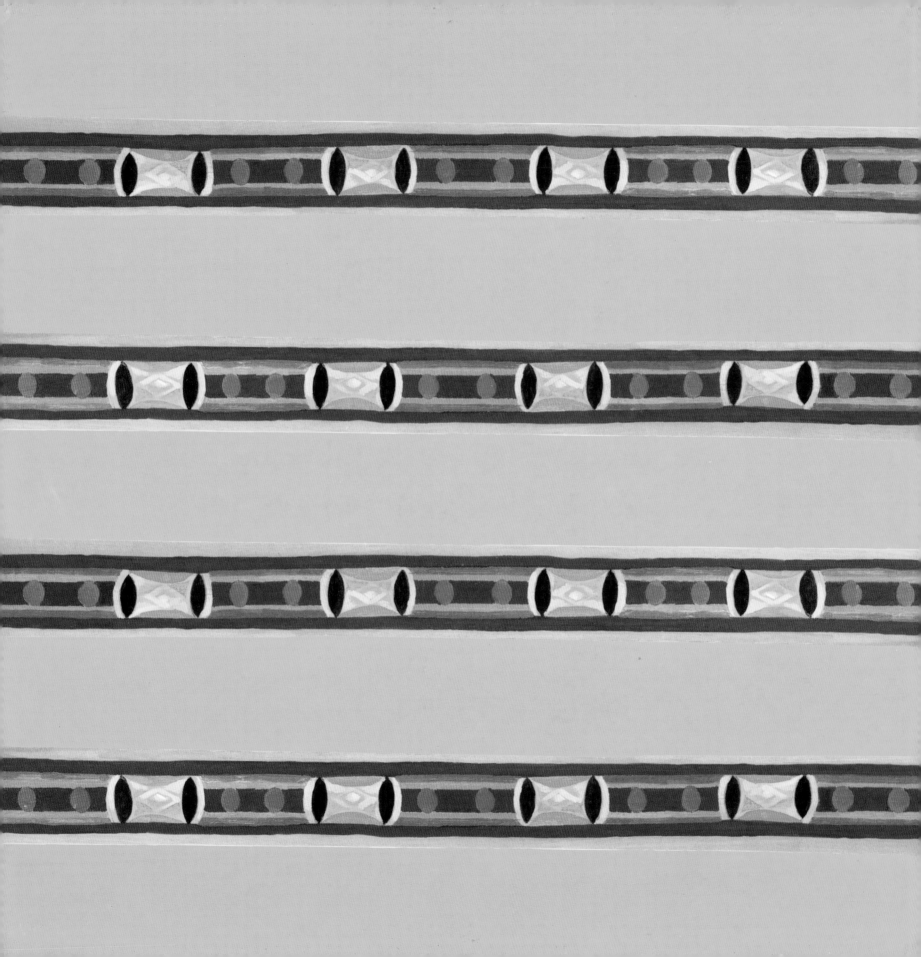